Zapato Power
FREDDIE RAMOS
MAKES A SPLASH

No Lo
Washo

D0972212

JACQUELINE JULES   art by MIGUEL BENÍTEZ

Albert Whitman & Company
Chicago, Illinois

Don't miss the first three **Zapato Power** books!

Freddie Ramos Takes Off
Freddie Ramos Springs into Action
Freddie Ramos Zooms to the Rescue
by Jacqueline Jules
illustrated by Miguel Benítez

Library of Congress Cataloging-in-Publication Data

Jules, Jacqueline.
Zapato power : Freddie Ramos makes a splash / by Jacqueline Jules ; illustrated
by Miguel Benítez.
p. cm.
Summary: Freddie Ramos uses his super powers to give himself courage to learn
how to swim and to deal with a new neighbor who is a bully.
ISBN 978-0-8075-9485-8 (hardcover)
ISBN 978-0-8075-9486-5 (paperback)
[1. Superheroes—Fiction. 2. Sneakers—Fiction. 3. Camps—Fiction. 4. Bullies—
Fiction. 5. Hispanic Americans—Fiction.] I. Benítez, Miguel, ill. II. Title. III.
Title: Freddie Ramos makes a splash.
PZ7.J92947Zah 2012
[Fic]—dc23
2011016027

Printed in China.
10 9 8 7 6 5 4 3 2 1 NP 18 17 16 15 14 13

The design is by Nick Tiemersma.

For more information about Albert Whitman & Company,
visit our web site at www.albertwhitman.com.

To the KidLit Blogging Community: Thank You! —JJ

CONTENTS

1. Bubble Gum on the Sidewalk

It was so hot, I was melting into the sidewalk, like the purple bubble gum I stepped in on my way home from summer camp.

"ICK!" I was stuck.

My shoes were special. They gave me Zapato Power, the power to run faster

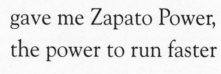

A little grape bubble gum shouldn't have stopped me.

I bent down and pulled on my right foot. That unstuck my sneaker but unbalanced me. SPLAT!

My bottom hit the ground, and I felt something underneath me. I hoped it wasn't dog poop.

Sometimes superheroes have to be brave even when they don't want to be. I looked to see what I was sitting on.

Luckily, it wasn't dog poop. It was a pink wallet.

Who dropped a wallet? I opened it. Superheroes don't steal, but they

do snoop. There were two twenty-dollar bills inside. Wow!

Before I could find out more, a  girl with short, dark hair rode up on a green bike. Maybe the wallet was hers.

"Is this yours?" I asked, holding it out.

"NO!" she said, swiping the wallet from my hand. "But it's not yours either."

The girl rode off on her green bike. I couldn't let her get away with that! I had Zapato Power, and I could outrun a bike.

I stood up and put on my silver goggles, the ones that almost make me look like a superhero. Then I pressed the button on my purple wristband, the one that controls my Zapato Power. I was ready to catch that girl crook in the blink of an eye.

ZOOM! ZOOM! ZaPaTO!

I fell backward on my bottom again.

sPLaT!

Huh? My Zapato Power wasn't working!

"Freddie?" a deep voice called. "What happened?"

It was Mr. Vaslov. He's the man who takes care of Starwood Park, where I live. He's also the only other person who knows about my Zapato Power, because he's the guy who made my special shoes.

"I don't know," I said, looking at the purple wad of bubble gum underneath my right sneaker.

Mr. Vaslov took a flat blade out of his pocket. He's an inventor and a fixer, so he always has tools handy.

"Looks like you need a clean-up," he said.

While Mr. Vaslov scraped the gum, I told him about the girl on the green bike.

"I think I've seen her before," I said.

"Maybe she goes to your school."

"Maybe," I agreed, trying to remember. She was bigger than I was, so I guessed she was older.

"There!" Mr. Vaslov said. "The gum is gone. See if you can run now."

I stood up on my purple zapatos.
I could feel them humming, itching
to race. And there was a girl on a
green bike with a stolen wallet. I
had a hero job to do.

ZOOM! ZOOM! ZAPATO!

2. The Girl on the Green Bike

When I run, smoke whooshes out of my shoes. No one can see me, but I can see just fine. The smoke from my super sneakers gives me Zapato Power eyes. That means I can see things way down the block.

ZOOM! ZOOM! Zapato!

At the very end of the street, I saw something shiny and green.

ZOOM! ZOOM! ZaPaTo!

I was there in half a blink, ready to face the girl on the green bike. But it wasn't her. It was my friend Geraldo on a green scooter. He opened his mouth like a fish.

"Hey, Freddie! Did you just step out of that puff of smoke?"

Zapato Power is the best thing in the world. But keeping it a secret sometimes confuses my friends.

I raced off, leaving Geraldo on his green scooter with his mouth hanging open.

ZOOM! ZOOM! ZAPATO!

The next green thing I saw was over by the entrance sign to Starwood Park. I zoomed over, hoping it was the girl on the green bike. Instead, it was my next-door neighbor, Gio, pulling a green wagon.

"Look, Freddie! Puppy likes to ride!"

Gio's little black dog, Puppy,
stood in the wagon. "Ruff! Ruff!"

Sometimes it takes more than
superspeed to catch a crook.

Sometimes, you have to ask
questions, too.

"Did you see a girl on a green bike?"

"Did she have black hair?"
Gio asked.

"Yes," I said. "When did you see her?"

"Right now!" Gio pointed over
my shoulder. "Behind you."

I turned around. The girl on the green bike was speeding past us.

ZOOM! ZOOM! ZAPATO!

She rode down the sidewalk fast, but that was no trouble for a guy with Zapato Power. In one blink, I was behind her, pushing a button on my wristband.

BOING!

My super zapatos do more than run. They can jump—right over the girl on the green bike. As I sailed in the air, I looked down to see something very lucky.

The bike had a basket, and the pink wallet was sitting inside, ready for a Zapato Power rescue.

I landed and ran back toward the girl on the green bike. She only saw me for half a second. I grabbed the wallet and zipped off in a puff of smoke.

ZOOM! ZOOM! ZAPATO!

3. A Not-So-Easy Hero Job

At the entrance to Starwood
Park, I stopped to look inside
the wallet.

Whew! The two twenty-
dollar bills were still safely inside.
Returning a wallet with missing
money wouldn't have made me
look much like a superhero.

But who did the wallet belong to? A library card gave me the answer: ADRIANA SOTO.

I knew Adriana. She was a counselor at my summer camp. She also lived at Starwood Park. This was going to be an easy hero job. I pressed the button on my wristband.

ZOOM! ZOOM! ZAPATO!

I raced down the sidewalk, looking for a tall girl with a long ponytail. She wasn't hard to find. Adriana was on her way home to Starwood Park, walking sideways, staring at the ground. She didn't

see the fire hydrant she was about
to run into. My hero job just got a
little harder.

ZOOM! ZOOM! ZAPATO!

I reached Adriana just in time to
bump into her. **OOPS!**

SPLAT!

We both fell over. The pink
wallet flew out of my hand.

"Freddie!" Adriana shouted.
"What are you doing?"

"Saving you from the fire
hydrant."

Adriana rubbed her elbow.
"Thanks. I guess."

"Are you all right?" a deep
voice said.

I looked up at Mr. Vaslov.
This was the second time in one
afternoon he'd found me on the
ground. Superheroes should fly,

not fall on their bottoms. They should also do a better job of catching people.

"We're fine," Adriana said. "But I lost my wallet. Did you see it?"

Mr. Vaslov pointed at something behind us. "Is it pink?"

"Yes!" Adriana leaned over and grabbed it. "Thanks! My wallet must have fallen out of my pocket. I'm glad to have it back."

I was glad Adriana had her wallet back, too. I just wanted to be the one to give it to her. Sometimes hero jobs turn out to be duds.

"How's summer camp going?" Mr. Vaslov asked.

"Freddie is one of my Tadpoles," Adriana said, "in swimming lessons."

The Tadpoles were the beginners. After that came the Frogs, the Dolphins, and the Sharks. One day, I wanted to be a Shark. But so far, all I'd learned how to do was cling to the side of the pool and kick my legs.

"Not enough kids at Starwood Park know how to swim," Mr. Vaslov said. "I'm glad you're teaching Freddie how to be safe in the water."

"Mrs. Barlow, the swim coach, wants to do more than that," Adriana said. "She wants to teach Freddie and lots of other kids to be lifeguards one day."

Lifeguards save people! That was for me. If I could learn to put my face in the water, I could be a lifeguard!

Adriana put her hand on my shoulder. "Tomorrow, Mrs. Barlow plans to spend extra time with Freddie while I help the other campers."

Extra time? Mrs. Barlow liked the way I kicked the water. She said if I'd just let go of the side of the pool, I'd do great.

"Good!" Mr. Vaslov said, just as his cell phone rang. "Leaking bathtub in 15C? I'll be right there."

Since Mr. Vaslov hurried off
to fix the bathtub, Adriana and
I walked home together. We said
good-bye at her apartment, and I
went on alone to 29G, where I live.

That's when two things
happened at once. I stepped in
another wad of grape bubble gum,
and the girl on the green bike
rode up.

4. POP!

The girl on the green bike parked in front of me, blocking my way.

"How'd you get that wallet out of my basket?"

Her voice sounded like a growl. I wanted to back away—nice and slow—the way I've seen people do on TV when they meet bears in the woods. But my shoe was sticky with bubble gum. I needed to clean it off first. Who was throwing gum on the sidewalk?

"Tell me how you got the wallet!" The girl leaned forward into my face. I smelled grapes. That answered one question. She was the one spitting bubble gum at Starwood Park.

I watched the girl's jaws move up and down, trying to remember where I'd seen her before. The gum made a popping sound under her teeth. Something inside me felt like it was being chewed up, too.

A purple bubble poked out of her lips, growing bigger and bigger, heading right for my nose.

If I didn't do something, I was going to have a sticky purple face! Could I jump? I pressed the button on my wristband. There was no tingling or humming in my feet. Zapato Power wasn't going to save me this time. I had to use brain power. "Watch out!" I shouted, ducking down low.

The grape bubble exploded all over her face, not mine. Whew!

"YOU'RE GONNA PAY!" she snarled, pulling purple stuff off her cheeks. "No one takes stuff from me!"

That's when my face got licked.

"Ruff! Ruff!"

Gio's dog, Puppy, came rushing up to say hello. Gio was behind him, pulling the green wagon. He looked at the girl on the green bike.

"Who are you?" he asked. "And why do you have a purple face?"

Gio is five, so he's still full of questions older kids are afraid to ask.

"None of your business," the girl on the green bike said.

She stared at Gio as if she was daring him to ask another question.

"**Ruff! Ruff!**" Puppy jumped in and out of the wagon, barking.

"You should keep your dog quiet," the girl said.

"How come?" Gio asked.

"Because I said so." She shoved Gio's shoulder and rode off.

Gio started crying. "I don't like her!"

"**Ruff! Ruff!**" Puppy barked.

Noise always opens doors at Starwood Park. Gio's big sister, Maria, came out.

"What happened?" she asked.

Maria was in my class during the school year. She was also in the Tadpoles with me at summer camp.

Gio told her about the girl on the green bike.

"I saw her through the window," Maria said. "Her name is Erika. The girls at summer camp say she's mean."

Summer camp? Suddenly, I remembered where I'd seen Erika before. She was a Frog! Her group went into the pool right after the Tadpoles!

5. Worried!

I felt as stiff as a telephone pole. Erika said she was going to make me pay. And I was going to see her the next day at summer camp!

"Freddie!" Maria called. "What's wrong with you? You're not moving."

"You look frozen, Freddie," Gio agreed.

Superheroes can't be scared, especially not in front of their friends. What should I say? I looked down at my feet and found an answer.

"My shoe has bubble gum on it."
I pulled it up to show the sticky
purple strings.

"I'll get a stick," Maria said.

A few minutes later, Maria had
helped me clean the gum off my
shoe but not the gunky feeling in
my chest. What was Erika going
to do to me tomorrow at summer
camp? Was she going to throw me
in the pool? I couldn't swim yet!

"See you tomorrow at camp,
Freddie!" Maria said. She and Gio
went into 28G.

I went home to 29G. The phone
was ringing when I opened the

door. It was my mom, calling to check up on me from her office.

"How was camp?" she asked. "Did you put your face in the water?"

"Not exactly," I said. "But I kicked good."

"I'll be home in one hour," Mom said. "Te amo. I love you."

An hour is a long time if you're worried about a bully. I tried drinking milk. I tried watching TV. I tried petting my guinea pig, Claude the Second. I even asked him what I should do about Erika at summer camp.

"Are superheroes allowed to hide?"

Claude the Second didn't have any answers. He just twitched his whiskers and looked cute.

Maybe Mr. Vaslov could help me. He had lots of good ideas. After all, he invented my super zapatos. I gave Claude the Second a carrot and left 29G.

ZOOM! ZOOM! ZAPATO!

Mr. Vaslov was not at his tool-shed, where he invented things.

He was probably still fixing the leaky bathtub in 15C. I turned to go there when I heard a rumbling noise. The metro train was passing Starwood Park on its overhead track.

My feet tingled in my super zapatos, itching to race the train. Even before I got my Zapato Power, I would run beside the track every afternoon with my arms out, pretending to be an airplane. That's why Mr. Vaslov gave me the super zapatos he invented. He figured that any kid who ran just for fun would

know how to take care of
special shoes.

ZOOM! ZOOM! ZaPaTO!

The second I started running,
I felt better. My whole body filled
with power as my feet moved faster
and faster, racing the train.

ZOOM! ZOOM! ZaPaTO!

Rápido! I zoomed ahead in a
swirling cloud of smoke until the train
was far behind. Zapato Power! I had

super speed! A train couldn't beat
me! Maybe a bully couldn't either.

I was ready for the next day at summer camp.

6. I Need My Goggles

In the morning, I dashed out of 29G with my white backpack on my shoulders and my purple sneakers on my feet. Maria met me on the sidewalk.

"Are you going to put your face in the water today?" she asked.

That was a good question. I

wished I had a better answer. "Maybe."

"Use your silver goggles," Maria suggested. "They'll protect your eyes."

"Good idea." My Uncle Jorge in New York had sent me the goggles for swimming lessons. But I'd been so busy using them with Zapato Power, I didn't always remember to use them for summer camp.

Maria and I walked down the street toward the high school, where summer camp was, until we came to Adriana's building. We saw her opening the door just as Mr.

Vaslov came around the corner. He had a pooper-scooper.

"Are you cleaning dog poop today?" Adriana asked him.

"No," he grumbled. "I'm cleaning bubble gum. Somebody at Starwood Park has been making a mess."

Erika! Suddenly, I realized something bad. Erika wasn't just a problem at summer camp, she was a problem at Starwood Park. She must live here, too. People were always moving in and out. But most of them were nice. They didn't mess up everything with sticky wads

44

of purple bubble gum that stopped
my Zapato Power.

"Can I help?" I asked Mr. Vaslov.
After all, I needed the same
thing—clean sidewalks.

He handed me his pooper-
scooper. "Thanks, Freddie!
You're super!"

I told Maria and Adriana to go
on without me, and I got right
to work.

ZOOM! ZOOM! ZAPATO!

In two blinks, I ran around all
the buildings with Mr. Vaslov's

pooper-scooper. Then I gave it back
to him with three more blobs of
purple junk inside.

"Who chews so much bubble
gum?" he asked.

"Maria says her name is Erika,"
I answered. "She's the girl on the
green bike."

"I'll watch out for her." Mr.
Vaslov looked at his watch. "You
better go, or you'll be late for camp.

"Don't worry." I waved. "With
my shoes, I'm never late."

ZOOM⚡ZOOM⚡ZAPATO⚡

Summer camp had two parts—before lunch and after lunch. In the morning, Adriana took us outside to play in a huge sandbox set up with a volleyball net. We pretended we were playing on the beach until we got sweaty. Then we went inside to make American flags for the Fourth of July. I painted popsicle sticks red, white, and blue with everybody else, but I kept my eye on the art room door. Was Erika waiting for me in the hallway, popping bubble gum? I reached down to touch my purple zapatos. It was a good thing I could run fast.

After lunch, we walked over to the pool. The girls went in through one door and the boys went through another. To go swimming, you have to change clothes in a locker room filled with wet towels.

I had a new bathing suit my mom got me for summer camp. She bought it on sale along with a white backpack  and flip-flops. Sale means I have to like the colors, even if the bathing suit is bright orange with big, green palm trees all over it.

"Hurry up, Freddie!" my friend

Geraldo called. "You're going to be the last one in the pool."

Geraldo didn't mind putting his face in the water for Mrs. Barlow. But I was happier putting my orange bathing suit on slowly, one leg at a time. After that, I carefully put my super zapatos away in my white backpack beside my clothes, my wristband, and my silver goggles. Just as I was finished and had no other excuses to stay in the locker room, a man with a rolling laundry hamper came in.

"Why are you in here alone?" he asked. "Aren't all the other kids swimming?"

"Sure," I said. "But I'd be happy to stay and help you pick up the towels."

The man shook his head. "That's my job. Your job is to learn how to swim."

He pointed to the door. I gulped and flip-flopped out to the pool.

"Come in the water, Freddie!" Mrs. Barlow called. "It's your turn."

The water looked too blue under the lights of the indoor pool. It also looked cold and wet.

"Freddie!" Maria said, jumping in. "Come on!"

I suddenly remembered that I had forgotten my silver goggles.

They were still in my backpack.

"Just a minute." I waved at Mrs. Barlow. "I'll be right back."

My flip-flops sure didn't go as fast as my super zapatos. And the floor was squishy wet. Worst of all was what I saw when I opened the locker room door. My white backpack wasn't on the bench anymore! It was missing!

7. Flip, Flop! Flip, Flop!

I looked everywhere. Nada. Nothing. All I saw were other campers' backpacks and a hamper filled with white towels.

There was only one explanation. Someone took my backpack with my super shoes! How could I be a superhero now?

I sat on the bench to think. Who could have done this? Only one person popped into my mind—Erika! She said she was going to make me pay. Did she know my backpack had my super zapatos, my goggles, and my wristband? Or did she just think she was stealing my clothes?

"Freddie!" Mrs. Barlow knocked on the door. "Swimming time is almost over. Did you find your goggles?"

When I went back out to the pool, I didn't have my goggles, my super zapatos, or my courage. Mrs. Barlow said we should try again next time.

FLIP, FLOP! FLIP, FLOP!

On the way home, my flip-flops hurt my ears. Every flip and every flop asked how I was going to get my super zapatos back. Where did Erika take them? Could I find out where she lived? Starwood Park had lots of buildings, and my only clue was purple bubble gum. I walked slowly, with my eyes on the ground, searching.

At first, all I found was Adriana. "Hey, Freddie!" she said. "What are you looking for?"

I wanted to tell her I was following a trail of bubble gum to find a thief, but then I realized I couldn't accuse anyone, not even Erika, without evidence.

"My white backpack," I said.

"Did you try the lost-and-found?" she asked. "Summer camp has a bin in the cafeteria."

The bin in the cafeteria was for lost things, not stolen things. Could I trust Adriana if I told her more?

"I don't think my backpack is lost. Somebody took it."

"That's what I thought about my wallet," Adriana said. "Then I decided to check and be sure I didn't just drop it. Accidents happen, Freddie."

"Thanks for the advice," I said, walking off. The trail could be getting cold. I didn't have time to waste.

At the next corner, I found a blob of grape bubble gum. Then, I found two more outside 25D. Could it be Erika's apartment?

I tiptoed into the bushes and peeked over the windowsill. Bingo! This had to be Erika's bedroom. There was a green bike inside! What about my backpack? I raised my head higher to search the room. I didn't find what I wanted.

"You little snoop!" Erika opened the window and hollered at me.

"If you don't get out of here, I'm calling the police!"

Superheroes are supposed to help the police, not be chased by them. I learned something: when I had to, I could still run fast, even without my zapatos.

The next day was the Fourth of July. We didn't have summer camp. Instead, I went to a parade with Maria and Gio.

FLIP, FLOP! FLIP, FLOP!

My feet made such a sad sound as we walked.

"Why aren't you wearing your purple sneakers?" Gio asked.

It was the last question I wanted
to answer but the only thing on my
mind. Sometimes you have to talk
over your problems with friends.

"I lost my backpack," I said.

"The new one?" Maria asked.

I nodded my head.

"What does it look like?" Gio asked.

"It's white," I said. "All over."

"Like a T-shirt?" Gio asked.

"Yes." Maria giggled. "Or a towel at the summer camp pool."

Everybody in the parade was happy to be celebrating America's birthday. There were marching bands and lots of red, white, and blue. Sometimes it was hard to see because so many people were watching. I would have had more fun if I wasn't wearing flip-flops. With Zapato Power, I could have bounced up high and seen over the crowd.

Where were my super shoes? Did Erika have them? When I thought about her, my stomach twisted up, just like it did when I tried to put my face into the water at swimming lessons.

At night, my mom took me to see the fireworks at the high school.

"The Fourth of July is my favorite holiday," Mom said as we sat down in the football seats. "It was your dad's, too."

"Really?" I liked learning stuff
about my dad. He was a soldier
and a hero for our country. We will
always miss him.

"Sí." Mom kissed my forehead.
"Your dad loved America's birthday."

A band played happy music.
Then the dark sky filled with

colors, bursting open like gigantic flowers. I looked over at my mom. Her smile was as bright as all the colors. We clapped and cheered together. For a little while, I forgot all my worries.

On the way home, Mom and I passed by the building with the summer camp pool, the last place I saw my white backpack with my super zapatos inside. Maybe it was all the noise from the fireworks, but something in my brain popped open with questions. What if Erika didn't steal my white backpack? What if it was just lost, like Adriana said?

How could a white backpack get lost? I remembered something Maria had said on the way to the parade. Suddenly, I had an idea.

8. Splash!

The next morning, I left 29G early, wearing my orange bathing suit with the palm trees. I was all ready to check out the pool before summer camp started.

FLIP, FLOP! FLIP, FLOP!

The flopping sound was so slow compared to Zapato Power. Would I ever be fast again? Or was I doomed to flip-flop around for the rest of my life? I hoped my brainpower was working, and that Maria had given me a good clue for finding my white backpack in the boys' locker room.

When I got there, I was happy to see the laundry hamper still in the corner, still filled with white towels, the same color as my backpack. Could my backpack be mixed in there by mistake? I sure hoped so. That's why I dumped the hamper over, just as the man who cleans things up came in.

"What are you doing?" he hollered.

He wasn't as friendly as the day my backpack disappeared. First, he made me clean everything up. Then, he grabbed my arm and marched me out to the pool.

"Is this kid with the palm trees one of your campers?" he asked my swim coach.

Mrs. Barlow looked at my orange bathing suit. "Yes," she said. "This is Freddie."

"Well, Freddie made a huge mess in the boys' locker room," the man said.

"That's not nice." Mrs. Barlow frowned and fingered the whistle around her neck.

"I'm sorry," I said. "I was looking for my backpack."

"Backpack?" the man repeated. "Was it a white one?"

"Yes!" I jumped up as high as I could in my flip-flops. "Where is it?"

"He'll tell you later," Mrs. Barlow said, putting her hand on my arm. "First, we're going to have a swimming lesson."

"But I need my backpack," I pleaded.

"Why?" Mrs. Barlow asked. "Does it have your goggles in it?"

I nodded my head. Superheroes

don't lie, but they don't tell everything they know either.

"If I had my goggles, I might be
able to put my face in the water."

"Then let's find your backpack."
Mrs. Barlow smiled.

She went with me to the lost-
and-found, the place where the
man who took care of the wet
towels said he put my white
backpack after finding it in the
hamper.

"Sorry," he explained. "I must
have picked it up with the towels
by mistake."

FLIP, FLOP! FLIP, FLOP!

My feet couldn't move fast enough. Was I really about to get my Zapato Power back?

The bin in the cafeteria was filled to the top. Underneath a couple of lost hats and a red T-shirt was a white backpack. I grabbed it and looked inside.

"My zapatos!" I shouted. "My wristband! My goggles!"

Everything was back. I could outrun a train or Erika's bicycle. I could help Mr. Vaslov keep the sidewalks clean. But before I did, there was something I had to do first.

I put on my silver goggles and looked at my swim coach.

"Are you ready?" Mrs. Barlow asked.

We walked back to the pool together.

SPLASH!

My goggles gave me the courage to jump in the water and get my whole head wet.

"Terrific!" Mrs. Barlow said. "Now put your arms out with your face down."

We practiced for an hour before summer camp. And when I came back with the Tadpoles after lunch,

I showed Maria and Adriana what I had learned.

"Freddie!" Maria shouted. "You're almost swimming!"

"Wow!" Adriana agreed.

At the end of the day, I climbed out of the pool, ready to be a superhero again. I got dressed and put on my purple sneakers to race home at super speed.

ZOOM! ZOOM! ZAPATO!

When I reached 29G, Gio and Puppy were playing outside.

"Look!" Gio said. "Puppy has a new toy!"

SQueak! SQueak! Puppy dropped a giant squeaky bone at my feet. I picked it up.

"Ruff! Ruff!" Puppy barked.

"He wants to play with you," Gio said. "Throw it."

Just as I raised my arm to throw, Erika came speeding by on her green bike. She swiped Puppy's bone right out of my hand and rode off.

"NO!" Gio cried. "Not fair!"

Erika didn't steal my backpack,
but she was still a bully. I had
my Zapato Power back—and my
courage. I could fix this.

ZOOM! ZOOM! ZaPaTO!

Erika turned the corner to
Building H, right past a wad of
purple bubble gum.

BOING!

I jumped over the gum and the
bike, landing a few feet in front of
her with my arms crossed. Erika
stopped her bike with a screech.

"Give back Puppy's bone," I said.

Erika opened her mouth so wide

her bubble gum fell out. I don't think she was used to people telling her what to do. She handed me Puppy's bone.

"**WaaaaaGH!**" came a little boy's voice.

"**Ruff! Ruff!**"

I heard Gio and Puppy back at 29G and turned around. Mr. Vaslov was walking toward us with his pooper-scooper.

"Puppy and Gio need you, Freddie," he said in his deep voice. "I'll take over from here."

He handed his pooper-scooper to Erika. "Clean up your bubble gum!"

Without saying a word, Erika took the pooper-scooper and got busy. Starwood Park's bully was under control—at least for the moment. I squeezed Puppy's toy and took off.

ZOOM! ZOOM! ZAPATO!

Zapato Power:
THE ADVENTURES
OF FREDDIE RAMOS

One day Freddie Ramos comes home from school and finds a strange box just for him. What's inside?

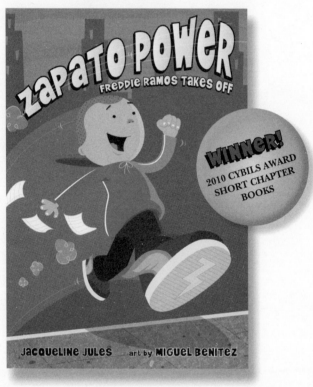

HC 9780807594803
$14.99/$16.99 Canada
PB 9780807594797
$4.99/$5.99 Canada

In this sequel, Freddie has shoes that give him super speed. It's hard to be a superhero and a regular kid at the same time, especially when your shoes give you even more power!

HC 9780807594810
$14.99/$16.99 Canada
PB 9780807594834
$4.99/$5.99 Canada

Freddie's super-speedy adventures continue—
now he has superhero duties at school!

HC 9780807594827
$14.99/$16.99 Canada
PB 9780807594841
$4.99/$5.99 Canada

Jacqueline Jules is the author of more than twenty books, including *Zapato Power: Freddie Ramos Takes Off*, which won a Cybils Award. She is also a poet, teacher, and librarian. Visit her at www.jacquelinejules.com.

Miguel Benítez likes to describe himself as a part-time daydreamer and a full-time doodler. He lives with his wife and two cats in England.